# Sleeping Beauty

Anne Walter and Laura Barella

# W
# FRANKLIN WATTS
LONDON•SYDNEY

# Chapter 1:
# A Princess is Born

Once upon a time, there were a king and queen who longed for a child. After years of waiting, they had a beautiful baby girl. "She is perfect!" smiled the queen, joyfully.

The king and queen were very proud of their daughter. They decided to hold a party to welcome her into the world. They invited all the fairies in the kingdom to come and bless her with gifts of beauty, wit, grace, dance, song and music. But they forgot to invite one fairy... and this fairy could be terribly mean when she felt jealous.

# Chapter 2:
# A Wicked Curse

The good fairies were just presenting their gifts when the mean fairy flew through the window. Everybody fell silent and a chill air blew through the room. The queen hugged the princess close to her, but it was too late. "You forgot me, but I shan't forget you!" hissed the mean fairy. "And you will never forget me again! My gift to your precious princess is this. When she has her sixteenth birthday, she will prick her finger on a spindle and DIE!"

With that, the mean fairy disappeared.
The king and queen were terrified for
their daughter. But there was one last
good fairy who was still waiting to give
the princess a gift.

"I cannot break my sister's curse,
however terrible it is," said the
good fairy. "But I can soften
it a little."

"Dear princess," she said gently, "if you prick your finger on a spindle, you shall not die. You shall sleep for a hundred years and be woken by a prince's kiss!"

9

# Chapter 3:
# The Curse Comes True

The princess grew into a beautiful, kind girl.
Everyone in the kingdom loved her – even
the little birds that flew down to eat from
her hand every morning.

Her mother and father never told her about the fairy's wicked curse. They didn't want to worry her. Instead, they ordered that every single spindle in the kingdom be burned, so that she could never prick her finger.

But on her sixteenth birthday, the princess went exploring in a tower she had never visited before. The tower was usually locked, but today, strangely, it was open. She spied a tiny room with the door left slightly ajar.

Inside sat an old lady at a spinning wheel.
The princess had never seen anything like
it and she was curious to find out more.
"Excuse me, what are you doing?" asked
the princess.
"I'm spinning some wool," said the old lady.
"Would you like to try?"

13

The old lady was really the mean fairy
in disguise. She made sure to prick the
princess's finger with the spindle as the
princess reached for it.

"Ouch!" cried the princess.

Then she fell to the floor in the deepest
of sleeps.

The mean fairy's cackling laughter rang through the quiet tower, but the princess did not stir.

# Chapter 4:
# The Castle Falls Silent

The king and queen were devastated.
They carried the princess to her bedroom
and lay her gently on the soft bed.

"We should have warned her never to touch a spindle," sobbed the queen. "When she wakes up in a hundred years, she will be all alone!"

Then the king and queen had an idea. They summoned all the good fairies to help them. "Please," they begged, "can you send us all to sleep for a hundred years too? Then, when the princess awakes, she will not be alone."

The fairies agreed, and they sent the king and queen into a deep sleep with the princess.

Then the fairies zoomed all over the kingdom, sending everybody to sleep. The whole castle fell silent.

A thick forest grew around the castle. Thorns and brambles crept up around the walls and doors. Nobody visited and the people inside stayed in their deep slumber.

# Chapter 5:
# The Prince's Adventure

A hundred years later, a prince rode to the top of a nearby hill. He had heard of a lost castle with a beautiful princess asleep inside. The good fairies whispered to him, encouraging him to visit the castle he could see peeping through the trees.

He rode deep into the forest, cutting through the thorns and brambles that lay in his path. Many hours later, he found a door to the hidden castle. Bravely, he opened the door and peered carefully inside.

He walked into the entrance hall. There, to his astonishment, he found the servants fast asleep! "It's true! The people here are enchanted! But where is the princess?" he wondered.

The prince looked all over the castle,
searching room by room, and finally he
found the princess. She still lay in her
deep sleep. He had never seen anyone so
beautiful, and fell in love with her at once.
The prince gently kissed the sleeping
princess's hand. She opened her eyes.
"You came at last!"
she whispered to him.

All around the castle, everyone woke up.

"What happened?" they wondered.

"What a strange dream!"

"I was just about to feed the dog!" said one.

"I was going to water the garden!" said
another.

Soon, the prince and princess were married.
They invited all the good fairies in the
kingdom and all the people who had shared
the princess's sleep. The castle rang with
song and laughter again and the prince and
princess lived happily ever after.

# About the story

*Sleeping Beauty* is a European fairy tale, first published by Charles Perrault in 1697. The Brothers Grimm also included a version of the tale in their collection of stories in 1812, called *Little Briar Rose*. In Perrault's version, there is a second part – where the prince's mother is part ogre and tries to eat the princess and their children! The royal cook deceives the mother and saves the lives of the children and princess. The Brothers Grimm stop the story with the arrival of the prince. The story of an enchanted princess is a common theme. It can be traced to a story called *Perceforest* of 1528 and further back to Norse sagas of the thirteenth century.

# Be in the story!

Imagine you are
the mean fairy.
How do you feel when
the princess falls asleep?
Are you cross that the
curse has not worked?

Now imagine you
are the prince and
you must write
a letter to the
good fairy. What
would you like to
say to her?

First published in 2014 by
Franklin Watts
338 Euston Road
London
NW1 3BH

Franklin Watts Australia
Level 17/207 Kent Street
Sydney
NSW 2000

A CIP catalogue record for this book is available
from the British Library.

The artwork for this story first appeared in
Hopscotch: Sleeping Beauty

ISBN 978 1 4451 3022 4 (hbk)
ISBN 978 1 4451 3016 3 (pbk)
ISBN 978 1 4451 3014 9 (library ebook)
ISBN 978 1 4451 3013 2 (ebook)

Series Editor: Jackie Hamley
Series Advisor: Catherine Glavina
Series Designer: Cathryn Gilbert

Printed in China

Franklin Watts is a divison of
Hachette Children's Books,
an Hachette UK company.
www.hachette.co.uk